KU-351-666

Peppa's Sandpit

Peppa and her friends are playing in the sandpit.

"This sandpit is our desert island!" decides Peppa. "We will live here forever."
"If we are going to live here forever I want it to be nice," says Suzy Sheep.

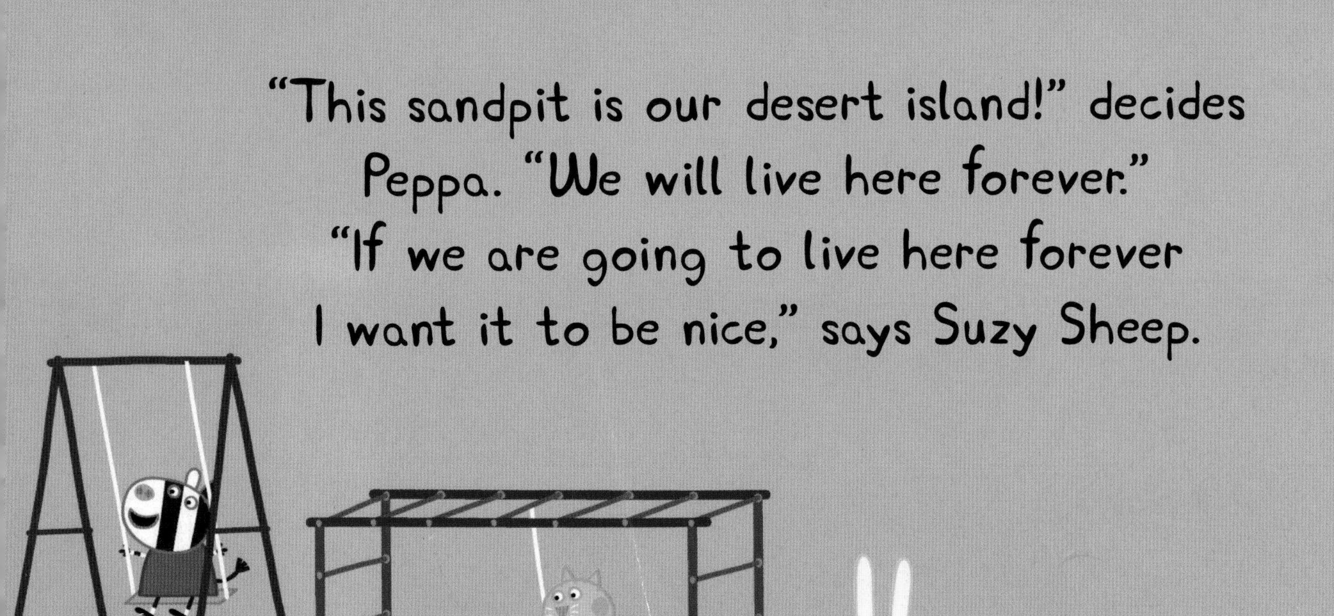

"The desert island just needs some houses," says Peppa.
"And roads!" barks Danny Dog.
"And shops!" says Suzy Sheep.

"Dine-saw!" shout George and Richard.
"Yes!" snorts Peppa. "The desert island can have dinosaurs, too!"

Emily Elephant looks at the desert island.
She thinks that it needs trees.
"Where are we going to get trees from?"
asks Suzy.

Danny Dog has an idea. "We have to drive big trucks around the world and look for trees!"

The dinosaurs guard the desert island while the others go to find some trees.

"Hello Mummy Rabbit," says Danny. "Have you got any spare trees?" Mummy Rabbit picks up some sticks. "There you go!"

Peppa and her friends drive their trucks back around the world. They plant the trees.
"There," says Peppa.
"We will live here forever!"

Candy Cat and Zoe Zebra
come to see the desert island.
"It would be really good if it
had a lake," says Candy.

Danny digs a lake. Now it needs some water. The children pretend to fly around the world looking for water.

Pedro Pony is playing on the roundabout.
"I know where there is pretend snow," he says.
"We can melt it to get pretend water!"

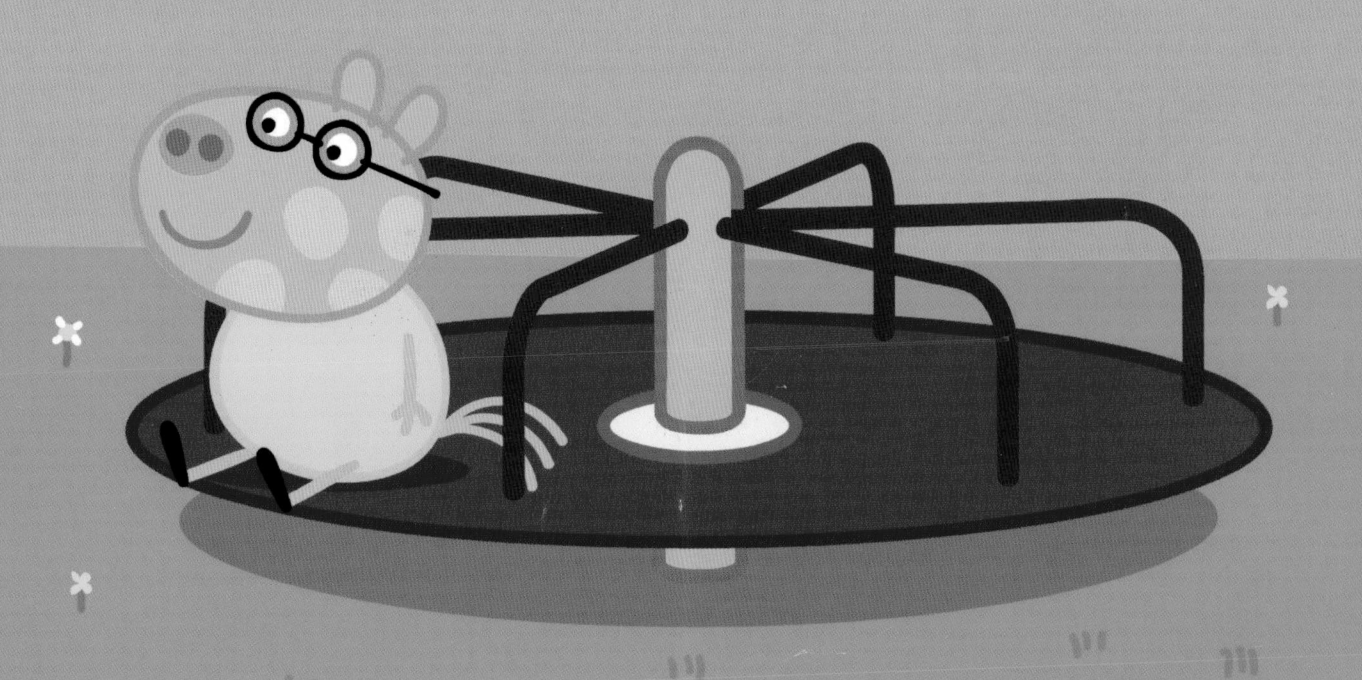

"This is a pretend mountain!" shouts Pedro.

Pedro climbs to the top of the mountain,
but there is no snow up there.
It has melted in the sun.
"Can't we pretend that it hasn't melted?"
says Suzy.
"No," neighs Pedro. "It has melted good
and proper."

Candy spots Daddy Pig. He is drinking from the water fountain.

"Can we have some water in our bucket please?" asks Peppa.

"Ho ho!" snorts Daddy Pig. "Of course."

Tee! Hee! Hee!

The children fly back to the desert island. Peppa fills up the lake.

"We've got water!" giggles Peppa.

Freddy Fox arrives. The desert island
is nearly ready.
"If only it had some flags," sighs Zoe.

Mr Fox takes a look in his van.
He has got everything in his van.
"How about these?" he grins.

Est. 2010
Yay!

Now the desert island is perfect. It has trees, roads, shops, dinosaurs, flags and a real lake.

"We can live here forever and ever!" cheers Peppa.
Snort!
Hee!
Hee!